THE POWER DOME

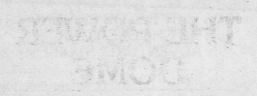

CHOOSE NOT ONE, NOT TWO, BUT 28
DIFFERENT READING ADVENTURES!

BANTAM BOOKS
NEW YORK • TORONTO • LONDON • SYDNEY • AUCKLAND

4 1974 02246 2805

THE POWER DOME

BY EDWARD PACKARD

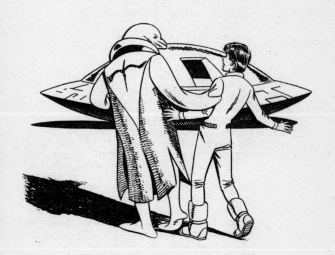

ILLUSTRATED BY ROY RICHARDSON

BANTAM BOOKS
NEW YORK • TORONTO • LONDON • SYDNEY • AUCKLAND

RL 4, age 10 and up

THE POWER DOME
A Bantam Book / August 1996

CHOOSE YOUR OWN ADVENTURE® is a registered
trademark of Bantam Books,
a division of Bantam Doubleday Dell Publishing Group, Inc.
Registered in U.S. Patent and Trademark Office and elsewhere.

Original conception of Edward Packard

Cover art by Samson Pollen
Interior illustrations by Roy Richardson

ISBN 0-553-56743-8

Published simultaneously in the United States and Canada

Bantam Books are published by Bantam Books, a division of
Bantam Doubleday Dell Publishing Group, Inc. Its trademark,
consisting of the words "Bantam Books" and the portrayal of a
rooster, is Registered in U.S. Patent and Trademark Office and
in other countries. Marca Registrada. Bantam Books, 1540
Broadway, New York, New York 10036.

PRINTED IN THE UNITED STATES OF AMERICA
OPM   0 9 8 7 6 5 4 3 2 1

THE POWER DOME

WARNING!!!

Do not read this book straight through from beginning to end. These pages contain many different adventures that you may have when you pass through a time portal to the future and find yourself enslaved by a menacing race of aliens. From time to time as you read along, you will be asked to make a choice. Your choice may lead to freedom or disaster. You may unlock the secret of the power dome, or you may arouse the suspicion of your captors and be condemned.

The adventures you have are the results of your choices. You are responsible because you choose. After you make your decision, follow the instructions to find out what happens to you next.

Think carefully before you act. You must find a way back to the power dome. But there is no way of predicting what dangers and terrors the future holds. Your best chance for survival will be to watch carefully, learning as much as you can about the strange new world of the future, until you see a chance to make your move. Then act quickly and decisively. The power is in your hands!

Good luck!

You're on a wilderness hike near the coast of Oregon. Your group has split up into pairs. Each pair is supposed to follow a different route through the forest, and then everyone is meeting back at the trailhead, where the charter bus is parked. The leader of the group, Dr. Gil Burns, is a geologist. You've learned a lot from Gil about how all the mountains, rivers, and lakes around here were formed.

Right now it's early afternoon. You and your partner, Nina Martineau, are in the thickest part of the forest. Nina is almost a year younger than you and looks even younger than that. She's the smartest kid in your class, but she's so busy counting the different types of birds she sees that she's no help in navigating through the wilderness. It's up to you to keep the two of you from getting lost.

Gil warned you that if you went off in the wrong direction, you might be stuck out here all night before they could find you. For that reason you're keeping one eye on where you're going and one eye on the compass. And when Nina goes running off, following a bird that flies by, you make sure she doesn't get out of sight.

About two in the afternoon you reach the crest of a ridge where the forest opens up. Ahead of you is a deep, broad valley, and beyond it a whole string of mountains. Beyond them lies the Pacific Ocean.

Turn to page 2.

2

Standing on a rock ledge about a hundred feet away is a huge elk with a full set of antlers. You tap Nina's shoulder, putting your finger to your lips. She gives a little gasp as she notices the elk.

"He's beautiful," she says.

The elk moves off into the forest. You and Nina sit on a rock and admire the view while you eat the sandwiches and fruit you've been saving until you reached a good picnic spot.

"Which way do we go from here?" Nina asks.

You check your map. The trail you're supposed to pick up should run along the floor of the valley below. You glance at your compass and point straight ahead.

"We can't go down there," Nina says. "The dropoff is too steep."

"I know," you say. "We'll have to cut through the woods and go about half a mile to our right. Then we'll come out where it's easier to get down."

"Look!" Nina is clutching your arm. A bald eagle is swooping over the valley. It banks sharply and swerves out of sight. "What a great bird! I could sit here all afternoon," Nina says. "But I guess we'd better go."

The two of you pack up your trash in a little plastic bag you brought and stuff it into your day pack. Then you lead the way through the forest, counting your paces and checking your compass so that you keep walking in a straight line.

Turn to page 4.

4

You've gone about half a mile when Nina suddenly stops. "Hey, we passed that a few minutes ago." She points at a huge fallen tree trunk.

"We sure did," you say. "There must be something wrong with my compass."

"Oh sure," Nina says sarcastically. She takes out her own compass. "Does yours show north that way?" she says, pointing.

"Yes," you say. "And that's also the direction the sun is in, which is impossible."

Nina gawks at you. "The compasses *are* off, then. But how can that be?"

You shrug. "Maybe there's a big iron deposit around here—that could do it. Anyway, we can't be too far off track. We'll have to find our way through the woods to where it's not so steep."

"Go through the woods without a compass?" Nina asks.

"I'll use the sun as a compass," you say.

"Lead on, then," she says.

You start forward into the thickest part of the forest, dodging stubs of broken branches jutting from the lower parts of trees.

"I think there's a clearing up ahead," Nina says, pressing ahead of you. She lets out a muffled squeal of excitement.

"What?"

She clutches your arm. "*Shhshh.* A spotted owl. See, on the highest branch. They're very rare."

Turn to page 47.

"Very well," this same alien drones in a low voice. "Then we may speak to you freely. You should know that the empress is very displeased that we have captured you. She had heard about you and the young girl you came with. You both appeared in good health. Do you understand?"

You nod. "Do you know where the girl is?" you ask. "She is my friend."

There is an exchange of high-pitched tones. Then one of them says, "We do not."

You wonder if Nina could have succeeded in escaping all the Alterians.

"The empress has offered a reward of a large pearl nautilus to anyone who brings you or your friend to her," the Alterian continues.

"So, are you going to trade me for a seashell?"

"No, we are not," one of them says. His eyes bore into you. "We have not broken the empress's grip on Teria by meeting her terms. We have a better way, and you will play a part in it. But make no mistake, if you are not perfectly loyal to us, you will suffer a terrible punishment."

"I understand," you say.

"Then, listen carefully to Umuru." He directs his gaze at a powerfully built Alterian, who then comes forward. He looms over you, his eyes training on you like laser guns.

Turn to page 107.

The robot leads you to a small air car parked nearby. The side panel slides open. "Get in," he orders. The tingling feeling indicates you'd better obey. But before you get a chance to climb in, another air car pulls up only a few feet away. An Alterian jumps out of the cockpit and knocks your robot guard over with a swift kick.

The robot is down but not out of commission. It sends out a pulse of sound so intense that it seems to burn into your brain. A moment later a brilliant red light flashes from its head.

The Alterian points toward the door of his air car. "Get in!" he orders. He hops in the front. He's trying to steal you from the others! With all the noise and confusion, maybe now's your chance to escape! You could hide out in the forest and make your way back to the dome. But you'd have to outrun the Alterian. You might get hurt, or be recaptured. It's hard to think. Is it worth the risk?

If you decide to obey the Alterian trying to steal you, turn to page 61.

If you try to escape, turn to page 31.

"Nothing in this place has been simple," you tell Nina. "And once we make our move, we can't turn back. Whatever the risk, we've got to think this through a little more."

"We need more information, and we need it fast," Nina says. "There are two ways I can think of getting it. One is from other humans, and the other is from robots. That old woman, Oomo, seems to know something the others don't. She must have learned a lot over the years. And she definitely took a liking to me."

"Still, a robot might have more facts," you say. "And not just any robot, one who's hooked up to central data banks like the HRS."

"Come to think of it, maybe we should try to find an Alterian who would help us," Nina says. "If we could find one who's sympathetic to us, they could take us right to the dome. We are in the elite corps. Maybe we could get the empress to help!"

"Then we'd be all set," you reply. "But I don't see how we could even get to see her again."

"Then why not the director of the center?" Nina says. "She seems really interested in humans."

You ponder this a moment.

Turn to page 110.

You are almost at your destination. And still nothing is showing on the rear display screen. The Alterians apparently weren't prepared for such a daring escape. Until you and Nina came along, the only humans around were so conditioned from centuries of being slaves that it wouldn't occur to them to try to get away.

A few minutes later the air car lands, setting down so smoothly you don't feel it touch the ground.

You want to give out a cheer, but Nina sits stone-faced. You're not home free yet.

"Thank you, robot," you say. "Please open the door."

The door slides open.

"What are my instructions now?" the robot asks.

"If we keep this craft here, they are sure to find it," Nina whispers.

She's right. "Robot, wait thirty seconds for us to get clear, then take off and return to your home base. Erase all memory of this trip."

"That is not a permitted command."

"What do you mean?" you blurt out. "Our master code is valid. You must follow our directions!"

"Wait," the robot says. "You are directed to wait. Do not leave. I have just been told to stand by for overriding instructions."

"*You're* directing *us* now?" Nina exclaims.

"Forget about that, Nina," you whisper. "Let's get out of here!"

Turn to page 54.

It takes a moment for you to catch your breath. You let Nina take your hand, hoping to calm her, though you've never felt so helpless in your life.

The acceleration ends. You let your tight muscles relax. The car must have reached its cruising speed. You try to get your thoughts together to make some sense of what's happening. But you can't seem to think straight. Your mind is blurring over—a jumble of distant sights and sounds.

Something in the air is affecting you. You don't know what it is, and there is nothing you can do about it. Dimly, you're aware that you're passing out.

You awaken in a large room filled with comfortable chairs, one of which you are seated in. To your surprise, you see about twenty other humans here, ranging in age from kids younger than you to adults old enough to be your parents. Everyone is dressed in matching dark blue body suits, including you! You shudder to think how some robot or alien must have changed your clothes while you were unconscious. You've got to get out of here!

You look around for Nina, but she's nowhere to be seen. Feeling a slight itchiness in your scalp, you pass your hand through your hair. You feel a little bump. A horrible thought occurs to you—the aliens may have implanted some kind of computer chip in your brain!

Turn to page 56.

Nina frowns. "Then have we gone forward in time, or backward?" she wonders aloud.

"I don't know," you say. "If Gil were with us, he could probably tell us whether Oregon used to look this way—before the mountains were formed."

"Or this might be how it looks in the future, millions of years from now," Nina says.

"This is kind of scary. Do you want to go back through the dome?" you ask.

"I suppose we should . . . except I'm more curious than scared." Nina has a funny look on her face. "You saw those birds. If this is the future, what other kinds of animals do you think we could find here?"

"Yeah," you say. "And I wonder if any people are still alive."

"Maybe we could do a little exploring if we stick together. Just until the daylight's gone," Nina says.

"We should be able to see a lot more from the top of that ridge. There might be a town there," you say. "I'll keep track of what direction we go in so we can find our way back. The ridge we're headed for is right in line with where the sun set. Coming back, we just have to go in the opposite direction."

Nina is looking to where the setting sun has slipped behind the hill to the left of the ridge. "Okay, let's just make sure we get back here before dark."

Turn to page 70.

By now the sun is down. Darkness is coming on fast, but you're guided by the first quarter moon glimmering through the trees. You and Nina spread out, hoping that one of you will stumble on the power dome.

You've covered about a hundred yards, making sure to keep within earshot of each other, when you hear Nina scream. You run toward her. The screaming stops. It seems to have come from behind a massive tree in front of you. You run around it and see Nina—gripped by one of the director's long, powerful arms. The other arm reaches for you. You duck and try to twist away. But fingers strong as steel cables curl around you, gripping you so tightly you can't even squirm. In vain you struggle to get away.

The End

"Because I wouldn't help the rebels," you reply. Leaning close, you ask, "Have you learned what happened to humans on this planet, and where these Alterians came from?"

"The humans around here don't know," Nina says. "Even ones who have been around for a long time. We were right. It definitely *is* far in the future. And something terrible must have happened to the human population. We are almost extinct!"

"I know," you reply. "There are only five or six hundred humans left on the whole planet! Do you think the Alterians are responsible?"

"I don't know whether they caused it or not," Nina says. "But they took over—that's for sure. These people have been enslaved for generations. Even I would be depressed. Only one of the people I met was at all friendly, an old woman named Oomo. She offered to give me music lessons."

"I think I saw her in the courtyard," you say. "She has a remarkable face."

"Have you learned anything else?" Nina asks.

You shake your head. "Not much. I wish we could access that HRS computer near the director's office. Then we might get some answers."

"Let's try it if we get the chance," Nina says. "The robot who gave me a tour said that the HRS is programmed to interface powerfully with humans, whatever that means."

Turn to page 64.

You pick up the nautilus, but instead of following Umuru's plan, you hold it out to the empress. "I cannot betray you. I am at your service," you say.

She takes the shell. At the same moment you feel a tingling—some kind of electromagnetic radiation coming from the empress. But it's not directed at you. It's a side effect of the electroforce she is aiming at the rebel Alterian. He collapses on the floor, as formless and helpless as a beached whale.

The empress draws your attention to her with a gentle tingling.

"You have shown your loyalty to me, and that you would not be enticed by the threats and promises of the rebels," she says. "If you wish, you may join the elite corps and be assigned to one of the noblest Alterian families in the land. Or, if you prefer, you can work in the school for humans, where you will teach other humans how to behave."

You don't like the sound of either choice. But that's not what's important. What's important is which choice is more likely to give you the chance to find your way back to the dome.

If you decide to help in the school for humans, turn to page 26.

If you decide to join the elite corps, turn to page 104.

"Blue, blue, orange, red," you say to the robot. "Now answer my previous question."

Instead of answering, the robot lets out a noise that sounds like someone running their nails down a blackboard, only much louder.

"Robot!" you scream. "Stop that!"

The sound ceases—it's no longer needed. Two huge guard robots with long steel arms are rolling rapidly down the hall, coming right at you. You yell at them to stop, but they don't seem to hear you. They are not the kind of robots that interface with humans. They are only programmed to cart them away.

The End

18

The director rises. Her legs have grown longer than you realized, and now she towers above you. "I want to see it, if it exists," she says. Then, in a harsher voice, she adds, "Do you know what the penalty would be if I were to take you to the Sacred Bay only to find that you're lying?"

You and Nina both nod. Actually you don't know what the penalty would be, but you can imagine it would be pretty bad.

The director stretches her newly grown arms. "Very well, I will take you there. For my own pleasure. And if the power dome exists, I may come back with you to see this earlier time—the time before we Alterians arrived at the Sacred Bay."

You are a little worried about the director coming back with you, but you can't back out now.

"We shall leave at once," the Alterian says. She strides out the door, with you and Nina following close behind.

Turn to page 25.

The following week you wait eagerly for Gil's call, but the days go by without any word from him. Another week goes by. Maybe he decided to dismiss your story after all. In a way you can't blame him; it was pretty incredible. You decide you'd better just forget about it and pretend it never happened.

Still, you can't stop thinking about it. Even if Gil didn't believe you, he did tell you he'd call. One day you phone the university where he teaches. The operator transfers you to another extension.

"Geology Department," a woman answers.

"I'd like to speak to Professor Gil Burns," you say.

"I guess you haven't heard," the woman says softly. "Professor Burns disappeared two weeks ago while hiking in Oregon. Hundreds of people searched for him, but not a trace was found. No one has any idea what happened to him."

You leave your number and ask that you be called if any information turns up, but you have a feeling it won't. You're almost certain that Gil found the dome, and that something very strange happened to him. You'll always wonder what it was. You resolve that someday, when you're older, you'll go back and check out the dome again yourself.

The End

"Let's duck into the cave!" you say, sprinting toward it. Nina is right behind you. You pause a few feet inside the entrance, waiting for your eyes to adjust to the dim light. You hear a squeaking sound ahead. Then, in the back of the cave, you see three tawny, scruffy kittens—or are they cubs? It's hard to tell. They look very young, but they are already bigger than full-grown cats. And they have long snouts like no cats you've ever seen.

Nina squats down to get a better look. "What *are* they?"

"I think we'd better get out of here," you say.

AWWRAAAARRRKKK!

You turn at the deep, snarling sound. The returning mother looks like a cross between a mountain lion and a grizzly bear, an animal that evolved long after you were born. She leaps on you first—you never learn whether Nina gets away.

The End

"This *is* the classroom," the Alterian says. "You will help Lara, the human you see there."

"But how can we teach them out on the playground?"

The Alterian looks at you as if you have asked a stupid question. "There is not that much to teach," he says. "Whenever you get close to one, say, 'The Alterians are great and good. Always obey the Alterians.' By hearing these words thousands of times over the years, the children come to understand the truth."

When you hear this, you resolve that you are going to teach these kids more than simple obedience. You are going to teach them to think for themselves, to understand that humans deserve the same rights as Alterians. You may risk your life in doing so. But even death is better than being a brainwashed slave. And that's what you would be if you obeyed the Alterians' tyrannous rule.

The End

"Let's talk to Oomo," you say. "You said she was friendly, and there's something intriguing about her. Maybe she could get others to help us. And we could even help some of them escape back in time."

"I'm not sure they'll even be interested," Nina says. "These people have been conditioned to think they're just slaves."

"I still think it's better than trying to talk to robots or aliens," you say.

Nina is looking out in the courtyard. "That's her," she says, pointing toward Oomo, who is still sitting on the bench where you first saw her.

"What's that she's playing?"

"They call it a kori. She hopes to be placed as a musician," Nina says. "The Alterians like to hear humans play koris, though the music is horrible, more like a squeal."

"Just what Alterians would love," you say. "They're squealers themselves."

"She wanted to teach me how to play," Nina goes on. "Come and meet her."

Turn to page 73.

A side panel in the aircraft slides open. "Get in the air car," the robot says. Its voice comes from a speaker in its neck but sounds amazingly human, just like the dolphin aliens.

You hesitate. Immediately you feel a tingling sensation behind your ears, which grows more unpleasant by the second. Nina is obviously experiencing the same discomfort.

"Get in the air car," the robot repeats.

You and Nina quickly scramble into the car, sitting in two of the four bucket-shaped seats. The seats are far too big for you, but almost instantly they contract to provide a tight fit. Webbed belts swing around and strap you in. The unpleasant feeling fades.

There are no windows—all you can see is the gleaming ceramic surface of the car's interior.

So far, Nina has seemed very calm, but now she cries out. "This is horrible! They're going to control us with electric shocks!"

You start to say something comforting, but a second later the side panel slides shut and you are pressed hard against the back of your seat. The air car takes off suddenly, accelerating at a tremendous rate.

Turn to page 10.

The director's air car is a luxury model and travels at supersonic speed. Less than two hours later, you, Nina, and the Alterian step out of it in a clearing at the top of a ridge. To the west, toward the setting sun, are the rippled waters of the Sacred Bay. You wish you had your compass but then remember that you traveled toward the setting sun from the power dome. Now the power dome is in the opposite direction. With a little luck you should be able to find it.

The director is peering into the woods as if trying to see through the trees. "So, must we walk through this forest to reach it?" she asks.

Turn to page 89.

"I'd rather help in the school for humans," you say.

"I am sure you will serve with honor," the empress responds.

The robot guards lead you gently away. They turn you over to an Alterian who takes you by air car to a clearing in front of a large white concrete building. The Alterian escorts you inside and leads you through a dining hall where food is served by robots. Then he shows you to the room where you'll be staying. It is small but clean. There's a sleeping pallet designed for humans on the floor.

"Where is the school?" you ask.

"Follow," he says, and leads you to a balcony overlooking an interior courtyard. You look down on a huge playground and dozens of human children. Most look about kindergarten age. Others are a year or two older. They are playing on swings, slides, and jungle gyms not very different from the kinds you played on when you were little. A young woman and two robots are watching over them.

"Where are the older children?" you ask the Alterian.

"There are none," he says. "Children finish school by the age of seven. Then they go into service."

You are shocked, but you pretend this is ordinary news. "Where are the classrooms?" you ask.

Turn to page 22.

Several birds fly past. They are twice as big as crows. A blue sheen glistens on their feathers. They perch in a clump of bushes a few hundred feet away.

"This isn't Oregon anymore," Nina says firmly. "There are no birds like that in all of North America. Look at the wingspan on those beauties."

You turn to look at Nina and notice the sun going down behind her, about to set. Just a couple of minutes ago it was early afternoon!

Nina looks around anxiously. "What's happened to us?" she cries.

"I don't know," you say. "Maybe the dome is some kind of portal used by aliens—a way of visiting other planets."

Nina shrugs, as if your idea is too weird to think about. She takes off the sweater she's been wearing, and you do the same. Suddenly it feels about twenty degrees warmer than before.

"Maybe we *are* on another planet," Nina says softly.

"I was thinking that," you say. "But that sun is the same size as ours, and look—" You point about ninety degrees to the left of the sun. A half moon is hanging in the sky, exactly like the one you're used to.

Go on to the next page.

Nina nods. "That's got to be our moon, all right. But we had a full moon last night. There's no way it could go from full to half in one day. I think we're still on Earth, but in a different time."

"Maybe so," you say.

Turn to page 11.

You make a break for it and immediately stumble. A tingling sensation rises from your fingertips to your armpits and quickly intensifies into a painful shock. The long arm of an Alterian seizes you, and you pass out.

You awaken standing up! You are in a factory of some kind, and without your willing it, your hands are fastening bolts on a metal fixture. The fixture moves along the line. Another comes along next to you. More bolts drop down from a chute. You start fastening these on, too!

How can this be happening? Desperately, you try to put your hands down. You can't. You try to run. You can't. You try to scream. You can't. You can't stop fastening the bolts. . . .

The chip implanted in your brain has been reprogrammed. Almost everything you do is under computer control. Mustering all your strength, you manage to turn your head partway to the side. What you see fills you with terror—dozens of coworkers lined up beside you. Robots, every one.

The End

The screen enlarges the scene as the air car descends toward a crystal dome in the center of the city. The palatial structure is surrounded by tile roads, gleaming and green as polished jade. Perfectly shaped trees line either side, spaced so as to afford a grand view of the palace from every approach.

Other screens show hordes of air cars, each marked with a blue horizontal stripe. "The empress's protection force," Umuru tells you. "They could blow us to bits—they *would* blow me to bits if they hadn't detected a prize human aboard."

The air car lands. The empress's guard of several dozen robots escorts your small party through the crystalline entrance to the palace, down a marble hall flanked with giant holographs of seashells. You and Umuru and his three robots pass through a great double door and enter the empress's reception chamber. All the while, Umuru keeps a long, molded hand resting on the back of your neck.

Go on to the next page.

The empress's robots train their little cameras on you, analyzing what they perceive and feeding it into computers you cannot see. You see no sign of hostility, but you suspect that Umuru was right in saying that the only thing protecting him is his ability to kill you.

You and Umuru stand waiting before the empress's empty throne. At last she appears through an entrance in the rear, a great, rounded Alterian with legs expanded so much that they interfere with each other's movement.

Turn to page 76.

"What island?" you ask.

Ignoring your question, the Alterian says, "I am aware that even young humans know that there are no shells on the island. But I see that you have a strong will, and that you are more clever than most. I will give you two shells if you promise to be loyal to the rebels." He picks up a second shell. His arm extending still more, flattening like the palm of a hand, he holds it close to you.

You stand there, wondering what to do. It's hard to take somebody seriously who's trying to bribe you with a couple of seashells—as if they were the most valuable things in the world. But you know this is no joke.

The Alterian holds the shells closer.

"Either you take these and promise loyalty to the rebels, or you will be sent to the island," the Alterian says. "Decide now, or we will decide for you."

If you insist on learning more of what's expected of you, turn to page 44.

If you promise loyalty in exchange for two seashells, turn to page 50.

You nod sadly. Everyone else in the group is leaving, too. In a minute or so you, Nina, and Oomo are left standing in the courtyard alone, except for the robots who come to take you away.

You are locked in a room overnight, and it is not until the next day that you learn your fate. An air car will carry you and Nina to a desolate part of the seacoast of the eastern sector. Then you will start your new lives: spending twelve hours each day walking along beaches, turning over boulders, sifting through pebbles, digging under driftwood, wading in the shallows, peering through the waters, endlessly searching for seashells in the sand.

The End

A red light flashes on the instrument panel. Signs, in the form of pictographs, appear on the display screens above them. You try to make out the meaning of some of the symbols, but the Alterian hunches over them, blocking your view. He's working some controls. The car shudders. You feel a sudden surge of heat.

The Alterian lets out a strange, high-pitched noise. On the rear screen you see streaks of light from the pursuing air cars. Your car veers sharply, then dips low. The pursuers instantly adjust their course. They're gaining.

Suddenly your car is diving, heading directly toward a cliff wall! But part of the cliff is sliding open. In a second, you're through the opening. Instantly the great stone-faced door closes behind you. A few moments later your air car comes to rest inside the hollowed-out mountain.

Through a side view screen you see your Alterian captor climb out. You watch him through the window making slight motions with his head. He seems to be communicating with two other Alterians who have come to meet him. A moment later the side panel slides open.

"Get out," a voice says.

You hop out onto the ground, slightly wobbly from your wild ride.

Turn to page 78.

The robot takes you down a long marble hall and through a huge doorway. In a moment you're outdoors in the sunlight, surrounded by high, gleaming white buildings with elaborate curved balconies on every floor. Alterians with their legs extended are walking on the streets or relaxing in their original form on their balconies. You watch one jump off, spread his short, stubby wings, and flop awkwardly but gently to the ground. The ones near you move their eyes forward to inspect you.

There are no vehicles on the streets, but you see a dozen or so air cars swooping along the broad canyons that separate each building.

Turn to page 6.

"Well, how can we get back to the dome?" Nina asks.

Oomo shakes her head.

"Or at least get back to the Sacred Bay?" you put in. "We could find it from there."

Oomo is silent for a while, her eyes resting on her kori.

"Is anything wrong?" you ask.

Oomo shakes her head and half smiles at you. "No, there is nothing wrong. It's just that it never occurred to me that this legend might actually be true!" She takes Nina's hand and then yours. "I am too old and weak for such a trip, but it would make me happy if you two could find your way back to your power dome. The Sacred Bay is thousands of miles from here. But I know a way for you to get there."

"Tell us," you urge her.

Turn to page 84.

You set a midrange altitude, set the course for due west, and pull down the yellow lever partway.

Instantly you're thrown back against your seat. The air car accelerates and climbs at a dizzying angle. In a minute, however, the car levels out and reaches cruising speed. It banks slightly and heads due west, just as you programmed it to.

The city drops behind you. Beneath you now is an endless expanse of forested hills, rivers, and lakes. You'd almost think you'd arrived on Earth before humans did rather than at some point in the distant future!

"Look at the rear screen!" Nina cries.

Two blue-striped air cars are pursuing you!

You apply full throttle. Nothing happens. You try gaining altitude. Again nothing happens. The pursuing craft are closing rapidly. You brace for a laser strike. It doesn't come. Instead, your air car slows and then does a wide turn, settling on a course that will bring it back toward its launch station. The Alterians have taken control of your air car. In a few minutes they will be controlling you!

The End

The woman turns away again and sits quietly, hands folded in her lap, head bowed, eyes shut. Many people in the room are sitting the same way, as if they are machines someone has turned off.

You touch her arm. "I'm sorry if I said the wrong thing. Please talk to me. I need to find the friend I came here with."

She looks at you intently. "You talk so strangely," she says.

"You seem to be talking strangely to me," you say. "I get the feeling you have been here all along—"

"Here in the holding chamber?"

"No, I mean here in this time, on this planet. You see, I just got here. Me and my friend Nina—"

"Just got to Teria?"

"Teria? Is that what you call Earth?"

She smiles without answering.

"We *are* on Earth, aren't we?" you exclaim.

"If that's what you call Teria."

"Then I am in a different time."

She leans closer and peers at you. "Yes, you pretend to be from a different time. As if you have been through a time portal. But that is just a legend." She squints at you. "You *are* a puzzle."

You almost tell her *she's* a puzzle, but there's no use arguing. You just want to find out what's going on!

Turn to page 101.

42

You decide to let yourself be assigned to a noble Alterian family, hoping that someday they will take you to the Sacred Bay. You hate to be separated from Nina again, but it seems the surest way for both of you to escape.

The following morning the director calls you into her office. With her are two adult Alterians and a young one, apparently their child. The child is just learning to expand his legs. He waddles in on what look more like flippers than real feet.

The older Alterians greet you in a friendly fashion, dipping their heads to you as they do to each other.

"You are lucky to be coming with us," they say. "Where we are going, humans are very popular. Our friends will want to see what tricks you can do. Can you stand on your head, for example?"

"Where is it we're going?" you ask, ignoring his question.

"To the Antarctic sector," your new master says. "This will be your new home."

"You mean we're going to live in *Antarctica*?"

Turn to page 88.

"Before I promise loyalty to anything I would have to know more about it," you say. "I don't even know what the rebels want!"

The Alterian's eyes, which were trained on you, slide back to the sides of his face, as if he's no longer interested in you. "You think I will offer a third shell?" he says. "No, that is too high a price to pay. You are clever, but you are too greedy. To the island with you!"

Summoned by some signal you are not aware of, two robots roll into the chamber. They lead you off, and you go willingly. You know you will be shocked if you resist. They load you into an air car. Three other humans are already there— an older man and woman sitting together and a teenage boy.

A robot straps you into a seat next to the boy. You wish you could see what's outside, but there are no windows. There aren't even any display screens.

Suddenly your straps tighten. The car accelerates so fast you're thrown back in your seat, unable to move or even talk. A few minutes later, the craft settles on course. You nudge your neighbor, though he seems to be half asleep.

"Did you refuse loyalty, too?" you ask.

"No," he says in a tired voice. "I have been loyal. But I dropped a rare pink scallop shell. They accused me of being a traitor to their cause."

"That's awful," you say. "Why do the Alterians make such a big deal out of seashells?"

Turn to page 83.

The moment of decision has come. You are supposed to take the nautilus and run. If you obey Umuru, and he succeeds in taking the empress hostage, perhaps he will be grateful enough to help you get back to the dome. At the very least, maybe he will help you find Nina.

But suppose he fails? Who knows what horrible fate might befall you? Maybe it would be wiser to run to the protection of the empress. She is the supreme ruler of the Alterians. If you could gain her favor, she could probably do much more for you than Umuru.

You can hesitate no longer. You must decide!

*If you carry out Umuru's plan,
turn to page 55.*

*If you seek the protection of the empress,
turn to page 15.*

But you're not paying attention. You're looking at something off to the right, through the trees. It's a dome-shaped structure about three feet wide and seven feet high. You take a few steps toward it. Its violet-colored surface is shimmering like water in a pond rippled by the wind.

Nina has followed you. "That's the weirdest thing I've ever seen," she says. "What makes it glow and shimmer like that? Do you think it's some secret government experiment or something?"

"Maybe, but wouldn't they have it guarded or fenced in?" you say. You move a little closer.

Nina steps closer, too, holding out her compass. "It shook the needle loose." She puts it down on a low flat rock and fiddles with the glass.

You look at her compass, then your own. The needle is still attached to your compass, but it's vibrating wildly. You extend your hand toward the strange surface of the dome. Nina clutches your arm. "Wait! It might be radioactive!"

You stop. You have a tremendous urge to find out what this strange material feels like. And just because something's magnetic doesn't mean it's radioactive. Still, maybe it would be wiser not to touch it, at least until you've talked to Gil Burns about it.

If you decide to touch the dome to see what it feels like, turn to page 79.

If you decide not to touch it until you've talked to Gil, turn to page 58.

48

"Let's try the HRS," you say. "I think that's our safest bet. It was built to serve elite humans. And it probably knows everything."

"Okay," says Nina. "Let's go take a look."

The two of you cut diagonally across the courtyard and go down a hallway to the alcove where the HRS is set up. Fortunately there are no Alterians or humans in the area. A small green light on the HRS's console means that it's up and running.

"Good morning, HRS," you say. "We would like some information."

"Certainly, that's what I'm here for," the robot says. It speaks in a polite, conversational tone.

"We would like to know how we can get to the Sacred Bay."

There is a pause, and you and Nina hold your breath, wondering if the HRS has access to such specialized information.

At last it answers. "You must give the authorization code."

Nina exhales loudly in frustration. "This is a dead end," she whispers.

"I'm not through trying," you whisper back.

Go on to the next page.

"HRS, state the authorization code, please," you say firmly.

Instead of saying no, as you expected, it replies, "If you ask that question twice, my instructions are to tell you that the code words are *blue, blue, orange, red.*"

Nina clutches your arm. "That's it!" she says. But you are not so sure—the robot answered in such an odd way.

*If you say the code words,
turn to page 17.*

*If you decide to ask some more questions
first, turn to page 100.*

50

"All right," you say. "I pledge my loyalty to the rebels."

The shells drop into your hand. You stuff them into your pocket. They aren't worth a cent to you, but to these creatures they're obviously valuable. Maybe they will come in handy.

"Very good," the Alterian says. "Come with me."

He leads you through catacombs cut through the granite mountain. The ceiling glows brightly, though you can't identify any light source. After about a quarter of a mile, the Alterian stops in front of a ceramic panel set in the side of the rock wall.

The panel slides open, and you follow the Alterian into a chamber where you see four similar creatures. About a dozen other rebels are lying in contoured lounges.

Their eyes swing toward the front as you enter.

Turn to page 60.

"Nina," you say, "I think our best bet is to get the director to help us. She's the only one here with any real power. If she's willing, she could take us to the dome herself in her air car."

Nina shrugs. "Maybe, if we could convince her that we're not crazy."

"It's worth a try."

The two of you proceed to the director's office. A robot outside scans you with its electronic eye. Apparently it decides you're harmless, because the door swings open.

The director is sitting bloblike in her lounge, no arms or legs showing. Her eyes move around to the front of her face, but not another muscle in her body moves. You wonder if she is listening to vibrations beyond the range of human hearing. They might be messages from other Alterians. They might even be music.

You wait patiently, not wanting to irritate her. Finally she begins to expand, first her back and then her legs and arms, so that soon she is sitting more the way a human does.

"It is unusual for a human to come into my office," she says. "What made you take such a bold step?"

"We came because we are not like the other humans here," you begin.

"What foolishness is this?" she says, continuing to grow her legs and arms.

"It's true!" Nina says. "We came through a dome, a portal from the distant past. And now we want to go back!"

Turn to page 82.

52

There are no roads or buildings in the countryside. Occasionally you see a river or stream wending through a valley. You pass over a large, sparkling blue lake. Luxuriant forests lie in all directions, but there is not a single sign of civilization. The countryside seems completely deserted. The Alterians must be city creatures.

"I thought I'd see villages and farms once we left the city," you tell Umuru.

"Food is made in factories, not on farms," he says. "There is no need to leave the cities, except to travel from one to another by air."

Your eyes are still fixed on the display screen. The air car has reached another city now—one similar to the one you were in before, but with broader canyons. The buildings are decorated with geometric shapes. The balconies are wider and grander. Great trees, hundreds of feet high, grow in the broad streets, their huge umbrella leaves giving shade to the balconies and plazas below. The air is fresh. You can see every feature in the finest detail.

"Is this the empress's city?" you ask.

He nods, imitating your human habit. "It was built by her mother a thousand years ago—in a better age. And there is the palace."

Turn to page 32.

Nina doesn't need any urging. She's out the door in a flash, and you are right behind her. None too quickly.

The door slams shut, almost whacking your rear end as you leave. You and Nina cut into the woods. You want to get where the robot's scanner can't detect you.

As soon as you've gone a few yards into the forest, you stop to think a moment. For the second time today, the sun is setting. By keeping it directly at your back, you know you'll be heading east toward the dome.

You and Nina hurry through the forest as fast as you can, desperate to reach the dome before darkness sets in.

There is only a little light left in the sky when you reach a clearing beneath the forest canopy. The dome is in the middle of it, exactly where you remembered! You race toward it and hear a roar overhead. An Alterian air car has arrived and is burning away overhanging branches, making an opening so it can land.

You and Nina fling yourselves into the dome.

A second later, the two of you step out into the same clearing in Oregon where you entered the dome. And you can tell by the position of the sun that the time is back to early afternoon!

"We can't let the Alterians follow us," Nina cries. "But how can we stop them?"

Turn to page 80.

You decide to stick with Umuru and his plan. You grab the nautilus and rush toward the door. No one moves to stop you, but the door slides shut before you reach it. You look around, expecting to see that the rebel Alterian has seized the empress. Instead he lies helpless in front of you, struck down by some silent blow.

One of the empress's attendants approaches you. You feel that tingling that will grow into an unbearable pain unless you do what he wants. You release the prize shell onto his outstretched hand and then turn to meet the empress's stare.

She speaks in a slow, deliberate tone. "See your master, fallen on the floor. Such is the fate of all who defy me, whether Alterian, human, animal, or robot."

You hear only familiar squeals and clicks as she issues orders to her robot guards. One of them grips you in its thick, encircling arm. He carries you down a long hallway and drops you through a small opening in the wall. You fall a dozen feet or so and land, bruised and bleeding, in a pit half filled with cast-off robots, some fairly new, others broken and rusting. Moments later another load is dumped on top of you, burying you forever.

The End

A robot like the one in the air car hands you a small bowl filled with orange-colored mush that looks like mashed yams. With its other pincers it deposits a metal spoon by your bowl. The humans around you are eating eagerly. Since you are very hungry, you take a bite. It tastes like a kind of pudding, not as bad as you were afraid it would be. You finish it off. You have a feeling it may be the only food you'll get.

"You are new here," the young woman sitting next to you says as she finishes off her bowl of mush.

"Yes," you say. "Where are we? I was afraid I'd never see another human again!"

"Why would you say such a strange thing?"

"Because of these robots, and those strange dolphin creatures. I thought I'd come to a place—or a time—where aliens had taken over the planet."

"Taken over?" the woman says. She looks at you curiously. "Have you been isolated since birth?"

"No! Why should you think that? I was with a group of my friends in Oregon only a few hours ago."

"Oregon? What sector is that in?"

"It's not in a sector, it's in a country—the United States!" You can't help feeling frustrated, and it seems to offend the woman. She looks away.

Go on to the next page.

"Tell me," you persist. "Where did you learn to speak English?"

"Is that what you're speaking?" she says. "I could understand and speak it no matter what it was. You know how." She taps a little bump in her head. It's in the same place where you felt the bump in your own head.

Turn to page 41.

58

You back off a step. "Guess you're right," you say to Nina. "Gil is a scientist. Maybe he can explain it. Come on." You start to turn.

"Wait. Do you have a camera?" she asks.

You shake your head.

Nina sighs. "Mine's out of film." You're not surprised. It seemed to you she was taking pictures of every bird she saw.

"Come on," you say.

Using the sun as your compass, you lead Nina back toward the valley. About twenty minutes later you reach the edge of the forest. Once again the valley is spread out before you, but the slope here is not as steep, and the two of you are able to scramble down a few hundred feet to where the terrain becomes more gentle.

Two hours later you find the trail marked on your map. Another hour's hike brings you to the head of the Jeep road. By the time you reach the trailhead, the sun has almost set. The chartered bus is waiting. You and Nina are the last hikers in.

Gil Burns is standing by the bus waiting. He takes a stride toward you when he spies you coming down the road. "I was beginning to worry about you two," he says. "What held you up?"

"I'll tell you," you say. "But I'm not sure you're going to believe it."

Turn to page 111.

60

You hear more high-pitched tones—tinglings in your ears. They must be talking to each other. The Alterian who brought you in nudges you forward until you're standing in the center of a semicircle, half surrounded by the others. You notice slight bumps in the surface of their bodies where their legs and arms, or wings, will grow when they want them to.

"So, you have sworn your loyalty to us?" an Alterian says.

"Yes," you answer.

"You must understand there is no turning back. Never even think of it," another says.

You nod.

Turn to page 5.

You decide you'd better obey the Alterian and get in the air car. A mechanism straps you in. The side panel slides shut. An instant later you're off the ground.

This time your view of the cockpit is not blocked. You can see the robot pilot and the Alterian next to him. You can even see through the front window. The air car is flying through a canyon between two tall buildings. A display screen in the cockpit shows the view behind you—the city of balconies and two silver air cars with blue stripes down the side surfacing above the rooftops.

You are thrown sharply against the door as the car veers down a side canyon, slipping sideways, nearly crashing into the balconies. The rear screen shows the blue-striped air cars making the same turn. You have a feeling that they are the police, and that you are with criminals. Well, as far as you're concerned, the police are criminals, too.

Suddenly your air car shoots out of the city. There are no longer any buildings or canyons beneath you, nor any suburbs or farms, just open countryside.

Turn to page 36.

"Let's wait here and see what happens," you say, trying to keep your voice calm.

The aircraft makes a final loop and then smoothly brakes, but instead of landing it rests in midair, hovering about twenty feet over your head. A panel on the side opens. Two creatures that look like malformed dolphins dive out. Their flat, stubby appendages look more like flippers than wings, but they provide enough lift to enable the creatures to flop safely to the ground. They stand facing you, balanced on their twin tails.

You and Nina stare in astonishment as the flippers seem to grow longer and narrower until they look like chubby arms. At the same time the tails flow into powerful legs.

On their new legs, the creatures stand at least six feet high. Their faces remind you again of a dolphin's, each eye looking out to the side. But this, too, quickly changes. Their faces flatten in a way that orients both eyes toward the front, so that they can look directly at you.

Their bottle-shaped snouts quiver slightly, like a rabbit's. You would laugh if you weren't worried about what they might do.

The creatures nod at each other, letting out clicks and high-pitched squeals. They seem as puzzled by you as you are by them.

Turn to page 94.

64

"These robots are a mystery, and the Alterians are an even greater one," you say.

"They act nice to us in some ways," Nina says.

"They think of us the way we do dogs and cats," you say. "Although the director seemed pretty nice. She introduced a film I saw."

Nina nods. "I passed her in the hall. She changed her face when she looked at me. It was almost like a human smile."

"She'd better watch out," you say. "The other Alterians will think she's weird, smiling like a human." The two of you laugh for the first time since you walked through the dome.

After eating a bowl of orange mush, you and Nina stroll through the little park outside the building. Two air cars are parked nearby, their robot pilots sitting at the controls.

"You notice something?" Nina asks.

"What do you mean?"

"There was a big guard robot standing in the courtyard earlier, scanning the air cars and the front gate."

"Maybe it's in the shop for repairs," you say, grinning.

"Wherever it went, it could come back anytime," Nina says. "Meanwhile, it looks like we could just walk out of here."

"Maybe we could even get hold of one of their air cars."

Go on to the next page.

Nina scowls at you. "Maybe they're not guarded at the moment, but when did you take flying lessons?"

"I didn't. I don't need them," you say. "The flying is done by the robot pilot. All we have to do is figure out how to give it directions."

"You make it sound easy," Nina says.

"There's a chance it could work. Then again, maybe we should take more time to plan out the details of our escape."

"Time would be nice," Nina says. "But we don't have much of it. They could assign us to Alterians at any moment. They'll probably split us up, and we'll never see each other again. We've got a chance to escape right now. Maybe we should take it. What do you think?"

If you decide to try to steal an air car, turn to page 116.

If you decide to take more time to plan your escape, turn to page 8.

66

"I can't stand the idea of waiting around for months. Let's organize a revolt now," you say.

"If that is your decision," says Oomo, "I'll call a meeting of all humans in the courtyard."

"Will the Alterians do anything when they see we're having a meeting?" you ask.

"I don't think so," she says. "These humans are soon to be assigned to different families all over the world. The Alterians will think we are just getting together to say good-bye. Wait right here. I will call them together."

You and Nina watch while Oomo goes to talk with the humans. First she approaches two men who are sitting on the other side of the courtyard. They nod and bow. You realize Oomo is highly respected by the others. When she returns a few minutes later, about fifteen or twenty other humans trail behind her. They gather in front of you.

Oomo faces the group. "These two young people have come through the power dome, a portal from a time long since past," she says. "They come from a time when our planet was ruled by humans like us instead of by Alterians."

Some people start talking loudly, but Oomo quiets them with a wave of her hand. She nods at you, and you realize you are expected to speak.

You step closer to them, some old, some young, all staring at you as if you have arrived from outer space.

Turn to page 102.

"I have a feeling she'd catch up with us," you say. "We'd better wait."

In a few minutes the director comes up to you. "I'm ready," she says, glancing at her newly developed feet as if admiring how thick and tough they've become.

You and Nina lead the Alterian through the forest, but soon the sun sets. Darkness is coming on fast.

"Are you sure you know where you're going?" the director asks.

"I think so," you say. "The dome is in the direction exactly opposite the setting sun."

"I have a gyro compass in my brain," the director says. She takes the lead, stepping clumsily but quickly, with long, swift strides. It takes only a short while to reach the clearing you've been looking for.

You let out a whoop. "There it is!" you say.

The director walks slowly toward the power dome. She stands looking at it.

"I can't be sure it will take us back to our own time," you say after a while, "but I want to try it."

"Me too," Nina says.

Turn to page 75.

A robot reappears and asks if you're hungry. You tell him you are.

"That is well," he says. "Lunch period is beginning. Follow me." He leads you to a large, sunny room with a blue tile floor. Several dozen round tables occupy the room. Humans of all ages are sitting at them, in groups of four to eight. Other robots hurry back and forth, serving dishes of food.

You head toward a table with an extra seat. As you get closer, you let out a yell. Nina is there! She sees you and runs over to hug you.

You join her at her table, where she introduces you to the other humans, three teenagers and a middle-aged man and woman. They are not unfriendly, though they look rather distant. You are not interested in them anyway. You just want to talk to Nina. You would never have thought you could be so happy to see one of your classmates from school. But seeing her is like seeing yourself again—she is proof that you haven't gone completely insane. Oregon and home suddenly seem bright again in your memory. You've got to find a way back to that dome!

Turn to page 93.

The route you follow takes you through a stretch of woods, but after about ten minutes you come out in the clear. Ahead of you is a low limestone cliff. At the base of the cliff is an interesting-looking cave. You'd like to explore it, but the light is fading, and it's more important to get to the top of the ridge before it gets dark. You see what looks like an easy route up around the cliff. It shouldn't take long.

"Look!" Nina cries. "Over there."

You glance up where she's pointing at a small, disc-shaped aircraft swooping over you like a hawk.

"I thought flying saucers only existed in storybooks," Nina says. "But that sure looks like one to me."

"Sort of like a Frisbee," you say. It's shaped so it acts as a wing but there are no jets or propellers. It loops in tighter circles as if homing in on you.

"It's going to land!" Nina cries. "What do we do?"

Go on to the next page.

You feel a rush of panic. Your first instinct is to duck into the cave. The aircraft looks too big to follow you through the opening. Then again, this might be your only chance to encounter an alien or a future human being and find out what's going on. Maybe you shouldn't pass it up.

If you say, "Let's duck into that cave," turn to page 20.

If you say, "Let's just wait here and see what happens," turn to page 62.

The two of you walk up to the old woman, who puts down her instrument and smiles up at you. Nina introduces you.

"Have you come for a kori lesson?" she asks.

"Actually, something else," Nina says. "My friend and I will explain. But will you promise not to repeat what we've said?"

"Everyone should have someone they can talk to without fear," the woman replies. "I will be that person for you, Nina, and for your friend."

The two of you tell the old woman the whole strange story of how you came through the mysterious dome and how you want to get back to it. Oomo listens carefully, looking a little skeptical, not that you can blame her. It must sound pretty crazy.

"You've got to believe us," Nina pleads when you finish.

The woman nods, reaches out, and touches Nina's hair. "Very few humans would believe you," she says. "Nor would I, except that what you've told me brings back the memory of a legend my grandmother told me when I was a child.

"According to the legend, there was a time before the Alterians—when humans ruled. Humans invented many wonderful things. They were great scientists. But then a plague spread across the world. Almost all the humans died." She looks off in the distance, as if trying to imagine what it was like for people caught in the plague.

Turn to page 96.

You are disappointed to hear this, but you haven't given up yet. Riding back in the bus, you sit next to Gil and try to convince him that you actually saw a shimmering dome. He stares straight ahead, tight-lipped, while you ramble on. Finally he turns and looks you in the eye. "You really *do* believe what you're telling me!"

"I do! It happened!"

"All right. Maybe it did," Gil says. "I'll tell you what. Write down the directions for me to get to this dome, and I'll hike up there next weekend and take a look."

"Thanks," you say. You start writing the directions. "I can't wait to hear what you think of it."

Gil reads over your directions. "That looks easy enough," he says. "I shouldn't have any trouble finding that ridge. And when my compass starts going off, I'll know I'm getting close, right?" He winks at you. "I'll call you to let you know what I find."

Turn to page 19.

The director turns and looks at you. "More than anything else," she says gravely, "I would like to see our Alterian forebears who lived in the sea."

"Well, come on then," Nina says. But the director hesitates.

"I thought I would want to come with you, but now I am not so sure," she says. "It frightens me to think of all those humans, with no Alterians to keep them under control."

"Well, it's up to you," you say. "And whatever you decide, thank you for your help." Then, nodding at Nina, you step into the power dome. An instant later you are standing back in the woods in Oregon. At least everything around you looks that way.

A second later Nina appears. She stares at you. "Are we home? And in our own time?"

"I hope so," you answer, but Nina has run into the woods along the edge of the clearing.

"It's still here!" she cries.

"What?" you say, hurrying up to her.

She grabs your arm and points to a low, flat rock. "My compass—just where I put it right before we stepped through the dome. Time hasn't changed since we left!"

Turn to page 99.

The empress waddles toward the throne. Umuru, rebel though he is, instinctively nods in homage as she passes. Once perched on the throne, her legs are swallowed up in her enormous body. Arms grow out. Her eyes train on you with such intensity that you feel like a flower wilting under the desert sun.

A servant brings the empress a green box covered in material that reminds you of moss growing in the shade of old trees. She opens the box and pulls out the pearl nautilus. It is breathtakingly beautiful—about three inches across, as delicate and perfect a thing as nature ever made. She places it on a table in front of Umuru.

Umuru nods in approval.

"Now deliver the human to me," she says.

Turn to page 45.

The Alterians train their eyes on you. You watch the arm of one of them expanding. In a few seconds it's much longer and stronger than the other. He grabs you around the waist and, with astonishing strength, lifts you high in the air. The others nod their dolphinlike heads.

"Put me down," you shout in frustration.

You're almost surprised when he does.

"Follow me," says the Alterian who grabbed you. He leads you into a huge hallway hollowed out of the granite walls.

You pass a table. On it is a row of seashells. They look like ones you've seen at the beach. Robots with armored jackets and strapped-on weapons are standing at each end.

The Alterian escorting you reaches out and picks up a shell. He holds it in front of you—it is not clear whether he wants you to take it or not.

"This will be yours, if you swear loyalty to the rebels," he says. "Will you swear?"

"What if I won't?"

The creature stares at you for a moment. You try to tell if he's surprised, angry, puzzled, or something else. But these creatures always look the same.

His answer is clear, however. "You will be sent to the island, as a worthless human."

Turn to page 34.

You can't resist touching the dome. You reach out and lightly brush the surface with the tips of your fingers. It's the strangest sensation you've ever had, as if the dome were made of liquid, sort of like warm water—except you can't see through it, and nothing splashes or spills out.

You try it again, this time sweeping your whole hand through it. Nina does the same.

The two of you stand back and look at each other.

"I don't think this was made by humans," you say.

Nina stares at the dome. "You think it's a UFO?"

"I don't know. But there's nothing else on Earth like this stuff," you say.

"I wonder what it is," Nina says.

"Maybe it's a listening post or something. I don't know." Again you sweep your hand through the surface of the dome.

Nina puts in her whole arm up to her elbow. Then she kicks the dome. Instead of making contact, her leg disappears into it until she pulls it out.

She glances at you anxiously, then reaches down and feels her leg, squeezing it along her calf. "It felt kind of funny, but it's okay. It's not even wet!" She prances around the dome, sweeping first her arm and then her leg through its surface. "Watch!" she cries. She leaps right into it and disappears!

Turn to page 91.

You wish you knew. You're so desperate you're willing to try anything. You pick up a rock and are about to hurl it but hold back, stunned, when you see the dome has started to drip. It's melting quickly, like an ice sculpture stuck in an oven!

Within about thirty seconds the power dome is only a flowing liquid on the ground. Soon it is just a wet spot. When you feel the ground, it seems dry. Then even the wetness evaporates, and the ground where it stood looks exactly like any other piece of the forest floor.

You have escaped from the Alterians. You will never see them or the future they live in again. It's a great relief, yet your joy is bittersweet. You're wondering who will believe you when you tell of your adventures. You and Nina are all alone in knowing about the frightening future that awaits humankind.

The End

"What you say reminds me of a legend I've heard," the director says. "A legend Alterians dare not talk about among themselves. According to this legend humans lived here before the Alterians arrived at the Sacred Bay. They came from a time in the past through a special portal called the power dome."

"It's true!" Nina cries.

"Legends are not truth," the director says in a sharp tone.

"It's not just a legend," you say. "That power dome is a few kilometers from the Sacred Bay. Take us there, and we'll show it to you!"

"It is close to the Sacred Bay? Most interesting," she murmurs. "No one is permitted to fly over the forest there."

"Even Alterians can't?" you ask.

The director gives you a penetrating look. "No. Especially the Alterians. It would violate the sacred law of pilgrimage."

You exchange glances with Nina, wondering what to say next. But the director continues, "It is interesting that you came to me when you did. The time has come for my own pilgrimage, my visit to the Sacred Bay." Her eyes are on you, but you have a feeling she's thinking of something else.

"If there *were* a power dome, and you got to it, what would you do then?" she asks sharply.

"We would go through it and back to our own time," you say.

Turn to page 18.

He gives you a strange look. "Why do you ask such an odd question? You can't be serious."

"I know it seems hard to believe," you say, "but I, well, I've been cut off from all knowledge about life here. I honestly don't know why seashells are so important. Would you explain it to me, even if it sounds stupid?"

He looks at you cautiously. "Surely you know that they are very scarce. We find them in the sand, sometimes buried very deep."

"You mean they are extinct? There are no more shellfish in the sea?"

"That's just part of it. The most important reason is that the shells are sacred."

"Thank you," you say, trying to be polite. "One more thing, if you don't mind my asking. What is this island that we're going to, anyway?"

"You pretend you don't know that either? All right," he says with a sigh. "The island is the prison where the rebels send humans who won't cooperate with them." Suddenly he grimaces as he's thrown against his safety straps. The same thing is happening to you. The air bus is braking sharply.

"You'll see it soon enough," he gasps.

Turn to page 108.

"By tomorrow you will be assigned to a family of noble Alterians. Most noble Alterians visit the Sacred Bay once every year. Their custom is to take their human slaves with them."

"Alterians visit the Sacred Bay? But we saw no buildings there."

"That is because it is sacred to them. When they come to visit, they stay at a communal dwelling up the river and take a boat down to the bay. Only one family is allowed to go at a time. They take their human slaves to witness their visit, so you would get to go with them. When they reach the bay, they swim in a big circle. Then they return to land. It means something special to them that I have never understood."

"But that means Nina and I will be separated again," you say. "And we'll have to work as servants for months before we get our chance to escape. Isn't there another way? Something we could do *now*?"

Oomo nods. "Listen carefully, then," she says. "You might be able to get the humans here to join you—you could promise them the freedom they would have by going back to the distant past. If all the humans here were united, you could overpower the robots and seize enough air cars to take those who wish to go to the power dome."

Go on to the next page.

"You think we could get away with it?" Nina asks.

"There is a chance," Oomo says. "The Alterians couldn't imagine such a revolt occurring. They have armed air cars, but until now they have only used them to fight rebel Alterians. You might be able to get through the power dome before they caught you."

Nina looks at you. "What do you think we ought to do?"

If you try to organize a revolt of the humans, turn to page 66.

If you let yourself be assigned to a noble Alterian family and wait until they take you to the Sacred Bay, turn to page 42.

"HRS," Nina says, "would you sound the alarm if we *commanded* you to open the director's office?"

"No," the answer comes back.

"Then we command you to open the director's office!" Nina grins from ear to ear. She has hit on another loophole in the HRS's defenses! The robot starts rolling down the hall, with you and Nina following close behind. Without any further instructions from you, it opens the office door, using a key embedded in its pincers. It rolls aside to let you in. You find the master code exactly where the HRS said it would be, behind the painting above the director's desk.

You and Nina hurry outside to the director's air car and climb inside. Using the code, you punch in instructions. A humming sound comes from the controls as the mysterious power source is activated.

"Robot," you say into the speaker. "Do you have human language capability?"

The robot remains silent. You wonder if it's sending some alarm signal.

Nina looks at you anxiously.

"Certainly," the robot finally answers.

"Very good," you say. "Do you have a navigational program that will take you to the Sacred Bay?"

"Certainly."

"Very good. Then, take us there immediately!"

Turn to page 114.

The thought of this makes you shiver. "Isn't it awfully cold there?" you ask.

"Cool, but not cold," the Alterian says. "All the ice is melted except on the mountains. No, I don't think you'll find it too cold. And you should know what a privilege it is to come with us. Our home is near the Sacred Harbor."

"Is the Sacred Harbor like the Sacred Bay?" you ask.

"You haven't heard?" the other Alterian asks. "Not all Alterians believe in the Sacred Bay. There are a few, like us, who believe that our ancestors arrived not at the Sacred Bay but at the Sacred Harbor."

"So you won't be visiting the Sacred Bay?"

The Alterian shakes his head. "Of course not. For our clan that would be a sacrilege."

The Alterian's mate steps toward you. "You shouldn't look so unhappy," she tells you. "Most humans would be thrilled to spend their lives in Antarctica."

The End

"I am afraid so," you say. "You can't land your air car in the woods."

"Then I must prepare for this," she says. "I will reshape my legs and grow tougher feet." She hunches on the grass and begins slowly reshaping her form. You and Nina walk off toward the edge of the forest.

"I've been wondering if we're doing the right thing," you say in a low voice, "letting an Alterian know about the power dome."

"She couldn't do much harm if she comes with us. One Alterian in a world of humans," Nina says.

"Yeah, but it will be like opening a gate. They might all come pouring into our time!"

Nina cuts you off with a wave of her hand. "I agree it's a danger." She glances back toward the director. "I don't think she's ready yet. We could give her the slip. She couldn't keep up with us through the woods."

"I'm not so sure," you say.

"Well, we've got to decide fast," Nina says.

You look back and see that the director is still working on reshaping her legs and toughening her feet.

If you try to give the director the slip, turn to page 112.

If you wait for her, turn to page 67.

"Nina, come back!" You pass your arm deep within the strange, liquid-like material, hoping to feel her. But you don't feel anything.

You take a deep breath and step into the dome after her. You see her at once. She's standing in front of you, staring out at the trees. You stare at them too. They are much larger than they were a moment ago. Their great branches overhang the clearing, blotting out the sky.

You glance back over your shoulder. The dome is behind you. In stepping into it, you stepped out of it as well, as if you'd passed through a door!

"This is so weird," Nina says. Her voice is shaking a little.

"More than weird!" you reply.

She takes a few steps and peers around a huge tree trunk. You join her and see that you are at a high rocky place where the forest opens up. The landscape stretched out before you is quite different than the view you expected. Ahead of you is a pair of hills. They are covered with tall trees except for low chalk cliffs near their bases that look like white scars in the forest. At the base of them you see dark patches that might be the entrances to caves. There's a low ridge between the hills. Beyond the ridge you can see a small bay, and beyond it the ocean.

Turn to page 28.

"No" the Alterian says. "Because I will stop them, and they will obey. I will have seized the empress while they are all looking at you! *She* will be our hostage. We shall take her back to our fortress. And her council will be obliged to meet all our demands."

"What *are* your—I mean our demands?" you ask.

Another Alterian answers from his lounge. "We demand the western continent for the rebels, an end to harassment, and half the shells in the empress's vaults."

"Very modest demands," the first Alterian says.

You are put into an air car, this one larger and fancier than any you've seen so far. There are three robots in the cockpit. You and Umuru are seated in the passenger compartment in adjoining lounges. The lounges look smooth and hard, but they feel soft as fur.

Display screens are mounted on the walls. Once you've taken off, they show the landscape passing beneath you—endless rolling hills, lush with vegetation. Where you might expect to see trees or grass stretches an unbroken blanket of pale green moss.

Turn to page 52.

You give Nina a quick rundown on your adventures. "I got to meet the empress myself," Nina says excitedly. "She asked me a lot of questions, and I played along with her, telling her how great her kingdom was."

"Shhh," you say softly. "Robots have big ears."

Nina giggles. In a low voice she says, "Anyway, I guess I put on a pretty good show, because she told me I would be an elite human from then on! And you, too! Why were you chosen to be elite?"

Turn to page 14.

"It's amazing the way they change shape," you whisper to Nina.

"Some animals on Earth—I mean in our time—change shape," Nina says. "Like frogs or fish that puff themselves up with air to look bigger and fiercer—but nothing like this."

"Maybe these creatures started out that way, and then evolved further," you say.

Then one of them speaks to you, in your own language! Its voice comes not from any movement of its mouth, but from somewhere within its head. "You are humans," the voice says without emotion. "You have dared to wander loose near the Sacred Bay. Therefore you will be sent to the distribution center for reassignment."

Nina clutches your arm. "How does it talk English like that?" You are wondering the same thing, but right now you're more interested in what the creature said.

"Who are you?" you demand. "We come in peace. Why can't you be friendly to us?"

There is no reply.

"How can you talk in our language?" Nina asks.

Still no reply. A moment later another aircraft swoops in from over the ridge and lands next to the first. The cockpit door opens, and a gleaming robotic figure steps out, about four feet tall with two mechanical-looking legs, two arms ending in crablike pincers, and an array of electronic sensors for a face.

Turn to page 24.

"Thousands of years went by," she goes on. "But the population never grew, and the few humans left lived in huts and foraged for food wherever they could find it. Then the Alterians came. They came out of the Sacred Bay. And they conquered the world. Nearly all the humans were killed. And those few who were not killed were made into slaves, as all we humans are today."

"So *that's* what happened!" you exclaim.

"That is the *legend,*" the old woman says. "Few people have heard it, but fewer yet believe it to be true. Most believe what the Alterians tell us—that they have always been here, have always ruled, and that humans are just the highest form of animal life."

"But that's not true!" you say. "The legend your grandmother told you is true—I can assure you!"

Oomo smiles slightly in a way that makes it hard to tell whether she believes you or not. "I would like to think so," she says at last. "But, whether or not it is true, what can I do to help you?"

Go on to the next page.

"Do you know anything about the dome?" Nina asks.

"Oh, that is a part of the legend I forgot to tell you. My grandmother said that a marvelous dome was built by scientists after the plague started. They wanted to escape to a later time, when the Earth would be free of the plague. It was the most amazing thing humans ever invented—they called it the power dome. They built it so that it would disintegrate after one round trip. That way no one could follow them if they wanted to return again from the future to their own time."

Turn to page 39.

A spotted owl flies out of a tree near you, and you and Nina hug and do a little dance—you're so glad to be back. Then you stand looking back at the dome, wondering if the director will also come through.

Suddenly she emerges, her huge body with its sprouted arms and legs climbing out before you. She lets out a series of whistles and clicks.

"What thin, spindly tree trunks," she exclaims. "Are we back in the time you came from?"

"I'm almost sure we are!" Nina says excitedly. "Follow us. We have to find the others in our hiking group."

"Nina, look!" you cry. All three of you stare in amazement. The power dome has begun to drip like rapidly melting ice. The director starts toward it. For a second you think she's going to go back in. But if that's her plan, she's too late. The power dome is melting too fast. In less than a minute it's completely gone!

You go to touch the wet ground where it stood, but the wetness evaporates even before you reach it. Not a trace is left of its presence.

"This is amazing," Nina says.

"This is awful!" the director moans. "I am lost forever. I can never get back to my own time!"

Turn to page 118.

"HRS," you say, "what would happen if I said the code words you just gave me?"

"My instructions are that if you say the code words, I am to sound the security alarm."

"When else would you be required to sound the security alarm?"

"Whenever you say certain things or ask unauthorized questions."

"Print out a list of them, please," you say.

"I am not permitted to do that."

You and Nina exchange glances. "Bummer!" she says. "Dealing with this robot is like walking through a minefield. We don't dare ask anything for fear of setting off the alarm!"

"I've got an idea," you tell her. Then, to the robot, you say, "HRS, if before each question I tell you that I am asking it only if it wouldn't cause you to sound the alarm, would that keep you from sounding the alarm?"

The robot does not reply for a moment; then, almost parroting your words, it says, "I would not answer the question, because you have told me not to answer it if it would cause me to sound the alarm."

Nina nods vigorously. "I think you've got something—we just have to put our questions the right way!"

"That doesn't mean we'll get the answer," you say. "But at least it's safe to give it a try."

Turn to page 106.

"What year is this?" you ask.

"L43. You did not know that?"

"No, they must number years differently now," you say. "Who are these aliens, anyway?"

"They are not aliens, they are the Alterians. They have been here all along. They are the masters," she says.

"The masters? How many humans are still living?"

"Five or six hundred," she says. "Our numbers are strictly controlled, you know."

You rub your eyes, thinking about how only a few hours ago, before you were transported in time, there were over five billion people on Earth. And now—five or six hundred! All slaves of the Alterians!

Another robot is gliding toward you. Its tiny wheels retract as it stops in front of you. "Your assignment has been made," it says. "Come."

Already you have that slight tingling feeling behind your ears, which you know will increase in intensity until you obey. "Where am I going?"

"You have been awarded to the Benami," the robot replies. "The Benami are important."

This is all you're able to hear, because the tingling is turning into pain. The robot is rolling out of the room. You hurry after it. The pain lessens as you catch up.

Turn to page 38.

"Friends, I offer you a chance for freedom," you begin. "If you will join us, we can overcome the robots and Alterians and take their air cars. Then we can fly to the power dome and all return to a time before the Alterians arrived, a time when humans ruled the world. You will at last be free."

"What is this word *freedom* you talk about?" a man calls out.

You are a little startled by his question, but an answer comes to you at once. "When you are free, it means that you can *think* what you want, and *say* what you want, and *live* where you want. It means—"

"How would we know what to do if we didn't have Alterians to give us work?" a woman interrupts.

"What the Alterians say is the sacred law!" another shouts.

"The Alterians would not approve of this!" a man says indignantly.

"But they *will* hear of it!" yet another man shouts. "I must tell them about it." He strides off.

Oomo runs after him a few steps, calling for him to come back, but he refuses to stop. She turns helplessly to you and Nina. "I am afraid I've misjudged my people. They cannot understand what freedom is. It doesn't mean anything to them. They think you are just troublemakers."

Turn to page 35.

"I would rather join the elite corps," you say.

"Very well," the empress says. "I'll have you sent to the Elite Human Processing Facility." She motions for you to go with her robots, who convey you by air car to a building unlike any you've seen before. It's about two stories high and is spiral shaped, coiling tightly around a large interior courtyard.

A robot meets you at the entrance and gives you a tour of the facility. He starts down a long hall and stops in an alcove by a gleaming silver cabinet. "This is the HRS," he says. "As you can see, it's not built on the human model, like many of the robots you've seen with arms and legs. It's a self-propelled computer that can receive sound and electro-magnetic transmissions. It processes all data relating to the service and care of humans."

Further on down the hall he stops again. "That's the office of the director," he says. "She is the Alterian in charge of everything at the center. But should you need anything, direct yourself to the HRS. He is connected to all central data banks and is more than capable of meeting your every need."

Go on to the next page.

He leads you on through a dining hall and into a courtyard. Several other robots are lined up against a wall, as if waiting to be turned on. About a dozen humans are sitting listlessly in lounge chairs, except for an elderly woman perched on a bench, plucking a stringed instrument of some sort. She is very old, but there is something about her wrinkled face that draws you to her.

Turn to page 115.

Over the next ten minutes you ask the robot a whole series of questions, each time telling it that the question doesn't count if it would cause it to sound the alarm. To each of your questions the robot responds that your question would trigger its alarm.

You stop a moment and look at Nina with exasperation. Then, unwilling to give up, you say, "Unless answering this would cause you to sound the alarm, tell us if there is any way we can get an air car."

"There is," the robot says.

"Unless answering this would cause you to sound the alarm, tell us *how* we can get an air car," you say.

Instantly it answers. "If you can get into the director's office you can get the master code to her car. The code is located behind a picture of a Tahitian conch."

This is exciting! Somehow you've found a flaw in HRS's security program, a chink in his electronic armor. But there is still one more hurdle to overcome. "Would you sound the alarm if we asked you how we can get into the director's office?"

"Yes, I would," the robot replies.

Your heart sinks. You're so close, but again your way seems blocked.

Turn to page 86.

"You will come with me to the empress's chambers," Umuru tells you. "We will demand to see the pearl nautilus before handing you over."

"But surely the empress must have more forces than you have," you say. "Won't they easily overcome you?"

"No. They will know that we will kill you if they try anything. And we know the empress's mind. She values humans almost as highly as shells. She will be careful to protect you."

"I understand," you say, even though you don't.

"I shall keep you close enough so they know that if they attack me, I could kill you in an instant," the Alterian goes on. "Then I will demand that the nautilus be placed in front of me and say that only when it is within my reach will I turn you over to the empress."

"But won't they grab you?"

"No. They won't dare risk damaging the nautilus. Now, here is what you must do. When I ask you to go to the empress, I want you to take only a single step toward her. Then take the nautilus and run for the door. The empress's eyes will turn on you. All eyes will turn on you. No guard, no robot, no matter how well trained, can resist watching a human trying to escape with a royal pink nautilus!"

"But won't the guards seize me before I can escape?"

Turn to page 92.

After the air bus lands, you follow the other humans out onto a small concrete strip. A blast of hot, wet air hits you as you step through the doorway. It must be over ninety degrees, even though it's lightly raining. The landscape around you is mostly dark volcanic rock, completely bare of vegetation. Gray, forbidding mountains tower around you, their peaks lost in clouds and mist.

A robot leads the group toward a cube-shaped cinder block building. It has openings like windows, but there is no glass in them.

You hurry and catch up with the boy you were talking to. "Hey, if it rains this much, how come there are no plants?"

"This is a part of history you didn't learn, but I have heard the story," he says. "The soil is radioactive on the island. This is where our human ancestors tried to destroy the Alterians with nuclear bombs. They killed many of them, but of course there was no hope they could resist them in the end. All they succeeded in doing was to make the island so radioactive that nothing would ever grow here. That is why the rebels send humans they no longer have any use for to this place."

Fear sweeps over you. "It sounds dangerous."

The boy reaches out and pats your shoulder. "It's more than dangerous," he says in a somber tone. "The Alterians call this the Island of Humans. But we humans call it the Island of Doom."

The End

"Whatever we do, we'd better get started soon," Nina says.

You nod, even as you're trying to decide what to do.

If you suggest trying to get information from the HRS computer, turn to page 48.

If you want to try talking to Oomo, turn to page 23.

If you'd rather try to get help from the director, turn to page 51.

You recount the whole story, with Nina adding details you skipped over.

"Did you get a picture?" Gil asks. You shake your head.

"I would have," Nina says, "but I ran out of film."

Gil shrugs. "Look, I make a point of keeping an open mind no matter how strange something sounds, but I have to think that you two cooked up this little story."

"We didn't!" you protest. "If you'll go back with us tomorrow, we'll show you. I'm sure I can find it again."

Gil shakes his head. "No can do. I have to be back at the university tomorrow."

Turn to page 74.

"Let's go for it," you say to Nina. You head into the forest at an angle, with Nina right in your tracks. The director apparently isn't watching; otherwise you're sure she'd yell at you. As soon as you're hidden by trees, you start jogging through the woods, heading directly for the dome. Nina follows. Despite her small size, she matches you step for step.

The two of you keep moving as fast as you can through the dense forest, always listening for the sound of the director behind you. Your hopes rise steadily as you put distance between you and the clearing.

Turn to page 13.

114

You are thrown back against your seat as the car lifts off the ground and accelerates, climbing rapidly over the city. A minute more and you're soaring over the vast, unpopulated countryside. You and Nina squeeze each other's hands in delight.

You have nothing to do but sit in your seat and hope all goes well as the air car streaks across what used to be America. By now darkness is setting in. It's amazing to see no lights below—there is nothing but wilderness beneath you.

No aircraft are following you—you've made a clean getaway! You are still very worried, however. The alarm has probably been sounded by now. You can only guess how long it will take the empress's attack craft to catch you. You keep your eyes fixed on the rear display screen, expecting to see pursuers at any moment.

The car streaks onward at tremendous speed, and though it was almost dark when you took off, it is now getting lighter again.

"Look!" Nina cries. The sun is peeking over the horizon. You watch it rising—in the west! Your car is traveling faster than the earth rotates, turning the clock back into late afternoon.

Soon afterward the craft brakes rapidly. Ahead and beneath you, you can see the Sacred Bay and the ocean beyond it, the late afternoon sun glaring off the surface. You think you recognize the two hills you noticed when you stepped out of the dome. It seems so long ago now.

Turn to page 9.

Your robot guide leads you on to your bedroom and leaves you there. You look out through the sole window, which overlooks the courtyard, then study the large pictures of seashells that decorate the walls. They are quite beautiful. But looking at them makes you sad. It's obvious that you have entered a world where even the luckiest humans are no more than pampered prisoners. Everything is chosen for them.

To your surprise you find an interactive video set up in your room. You start it up. An Alterian comes on the screen. "Welcome," she says. "I am the director of the Elite Human Processing Center. One of your privileges as an elite human is to see the world you will live in before you are assigned to it."

The director's image fades from the scene, and a film begins, giving you an air car view of mountains, plains, oceans, and deserts. You pass through Alterian cities, racing by the high buildings bristling with balconies and looking down on the Alterians' broad walkways and parks. In none of these views is there any sign of human life. You can hear music on the video, but it's more like random sounds than any recognizable melody.

Turn to page 69.

You approach the nearest air car. The robot pilot is sitting in the cockpit, waiting for instructions. You slide open the door and jump in beside it. Nina gets in back.

She leans over your shoulder. The two of you sit there a moment studying the controls.

"Let's hope it understands English," she whispers.

"I'm about to find out," you whisper. Then, in a louder voice, you say, "Robot, take off at once and head due west."

Nothing happens.

"It doesn't have a chip that lets it understand humans," Nina says. "I think you have to instruct it with the controls. That's how they start it." She leans forward and points to a yellow lever.

You study the instrument panel more closely. The aliens' written language is mostly pictographs. It's not hard to guess what many of them mean. There is a compass with a pointer, which you can move to indicate your desired course, and an icon of an air car, which you can move to indicate your desired altitude. An icon showing a jet blast probably indicates the amount of power to apply with the yellow lever under it. All in all, the controls the Alterians operate seem quite straightforward. The robot pilot does the hard part.

Turn to page 40.

"I'm sorry," you say, though the truth is you are relieved that hordes of Alterians won't be following you through the dome.

"Stay close to us," Nina says to the Alterian. "We'll take care of you."

The director's eyes go out to the sides, so that she reminds you of a frightened deer. "I'll be all alone in a strange world," she wails.

"You'll be all right," Nina says. She pats the Alterian's broad, curving back.

"I am afraid of how humans will treat me," the director murmurs. "They may make me a slave."

Like you made humans, you think. But that's not what you say. You say, "There's no danger humans will make you a slave. You will be treated kindly, I guarantee it."

You just hope you're right.

The End

ABOUT THE AUTHOR

EDWARD PACKARD is a graduate of Princeton University and Columbia Law School. He developed the unique story-telling approach used in the Choose Your Own Adventure series while thinking up stories for his children, Caroline, Andrea, and Wells.

ABOUT THE ILLUSTRATOR

ROY RICHARDSON studied at the Art Institute of Atlanta and Georgia State University. In 1983, he moved to New York to pursue a career as a comic-book artist. He has worked for both Marvel and DC Comics on such well-known characters as Captain America, Iron Man, and the Flash. His most recent work includes a Star Wars series for Dark Horse comics, done in collaboration with his wife, artist June Brigman. They currently reside in White Plains, New York, with their cat, Zeke.